Library of Congress Cataloging-in-Publication Data is available.
ISBN 978-0-06-195809-0

Typography by Dana Fritts and Brian Biggs
17 18 19 20   SCP   10 9 8 7 6 5 4 3 2
❖ First Edition

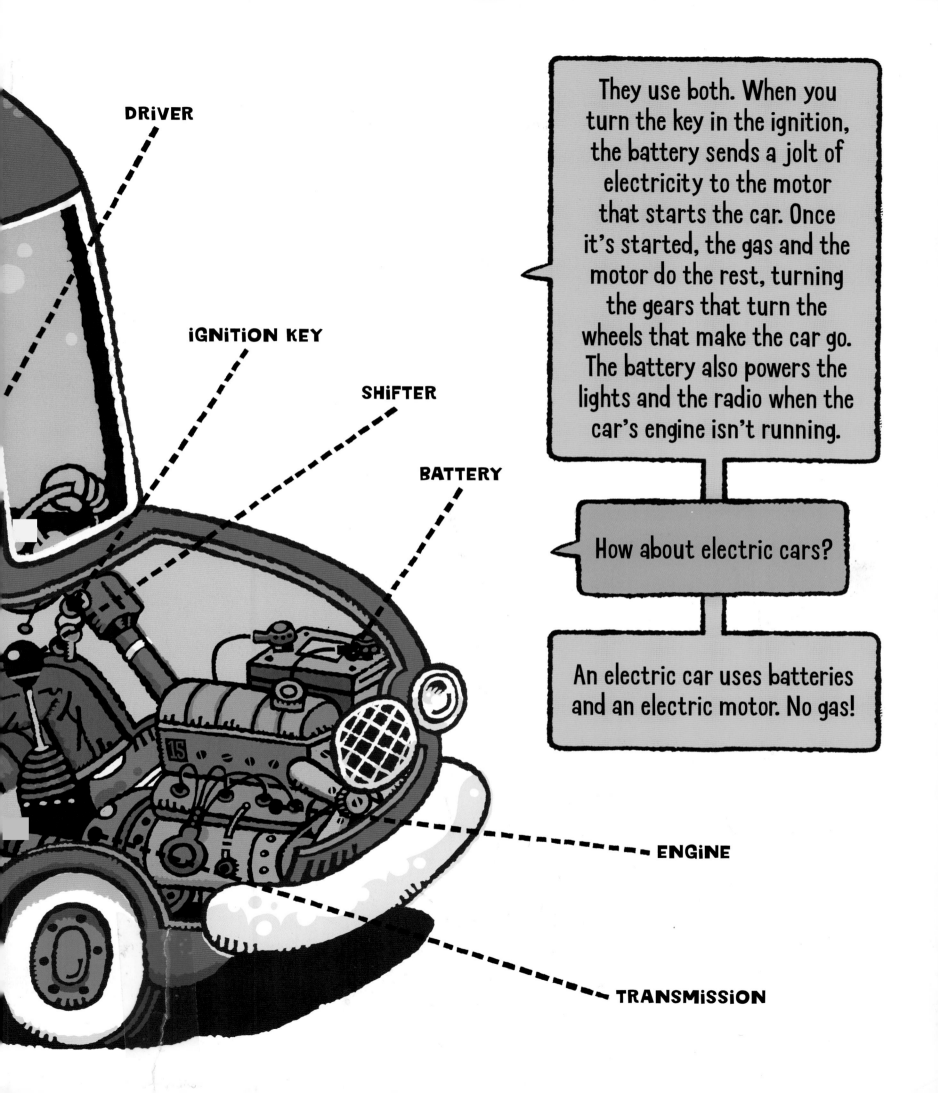

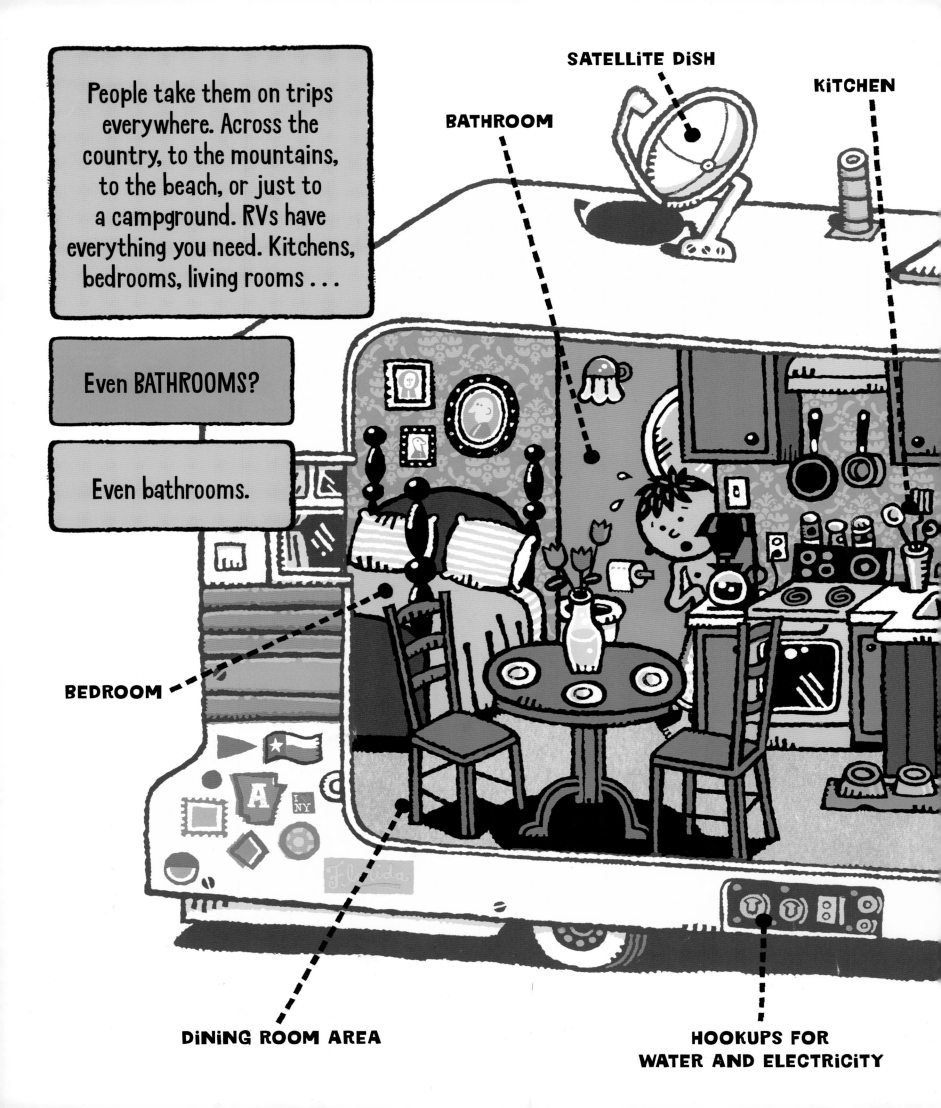

People take them on trips everywhere. Across the country, to the mountains, to the beach, or just to a campground. RVs have everything you need. Kitchens, bedrooms, living rooms . . .

Even BATHROOMS?

Even bathrooms.

SATELLITE DISH

KITCHEN

BATHROOM

BEDROOM

DINING ROOM AREA

HOOKUPS FOR WATER AND ELECTRICITY

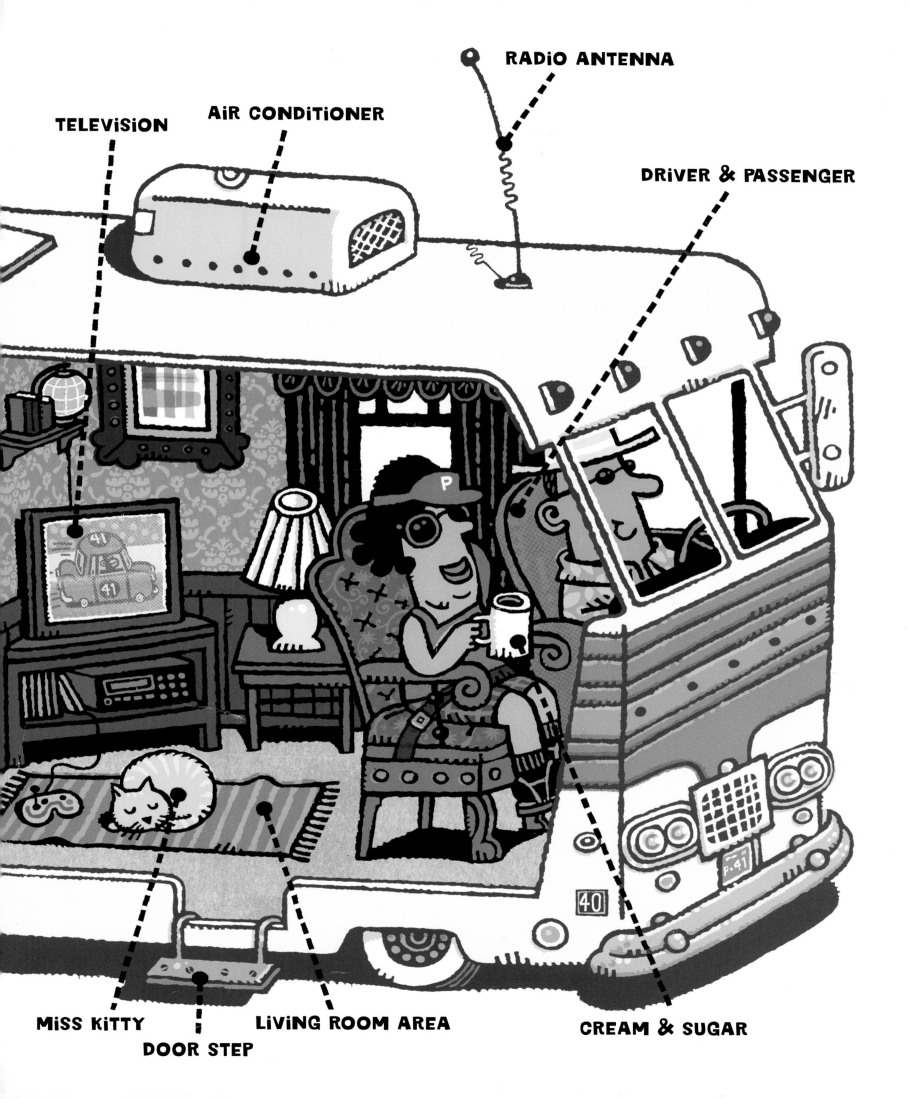

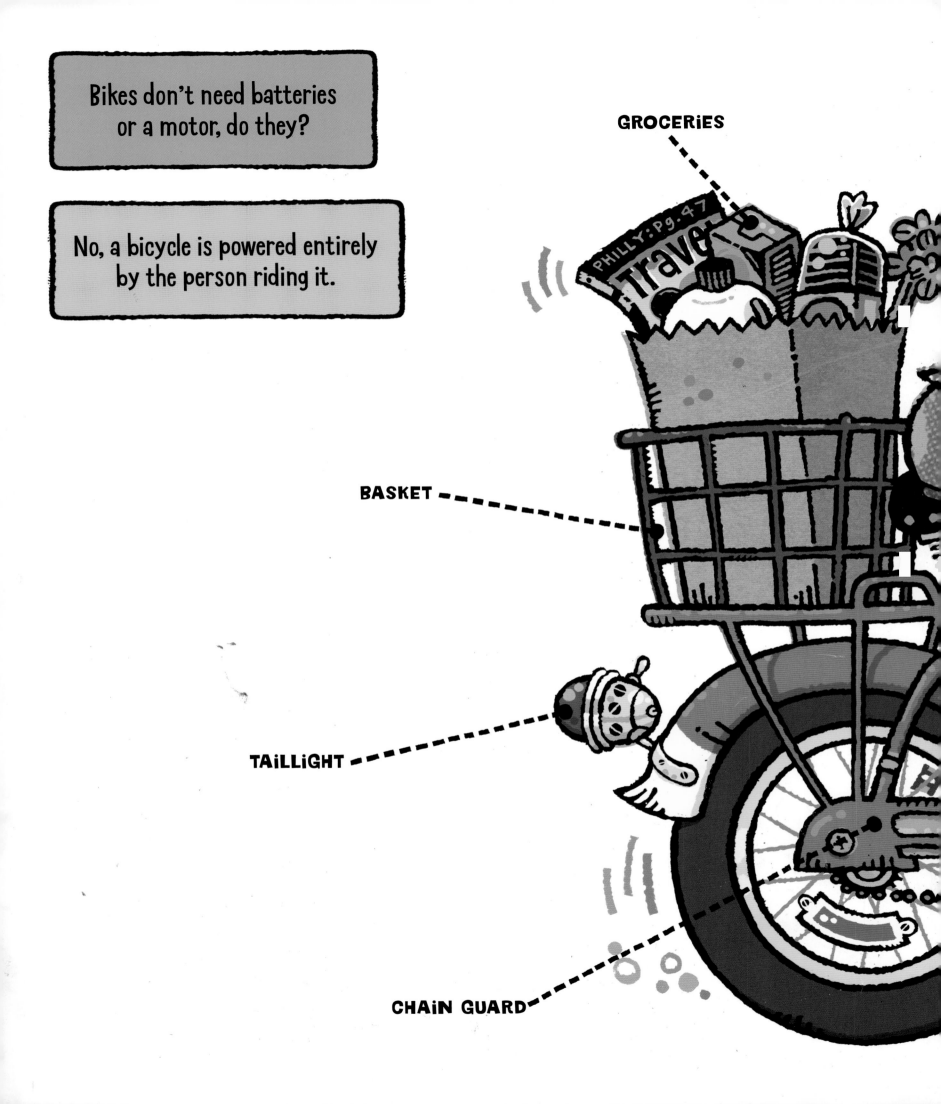

Bikes don't need batteries or a motor, do they?

No, a bicycle is powered entirely by the person riding it.

GROCERIES

BASKET

TAILLIGHT

CHAIN GUARD

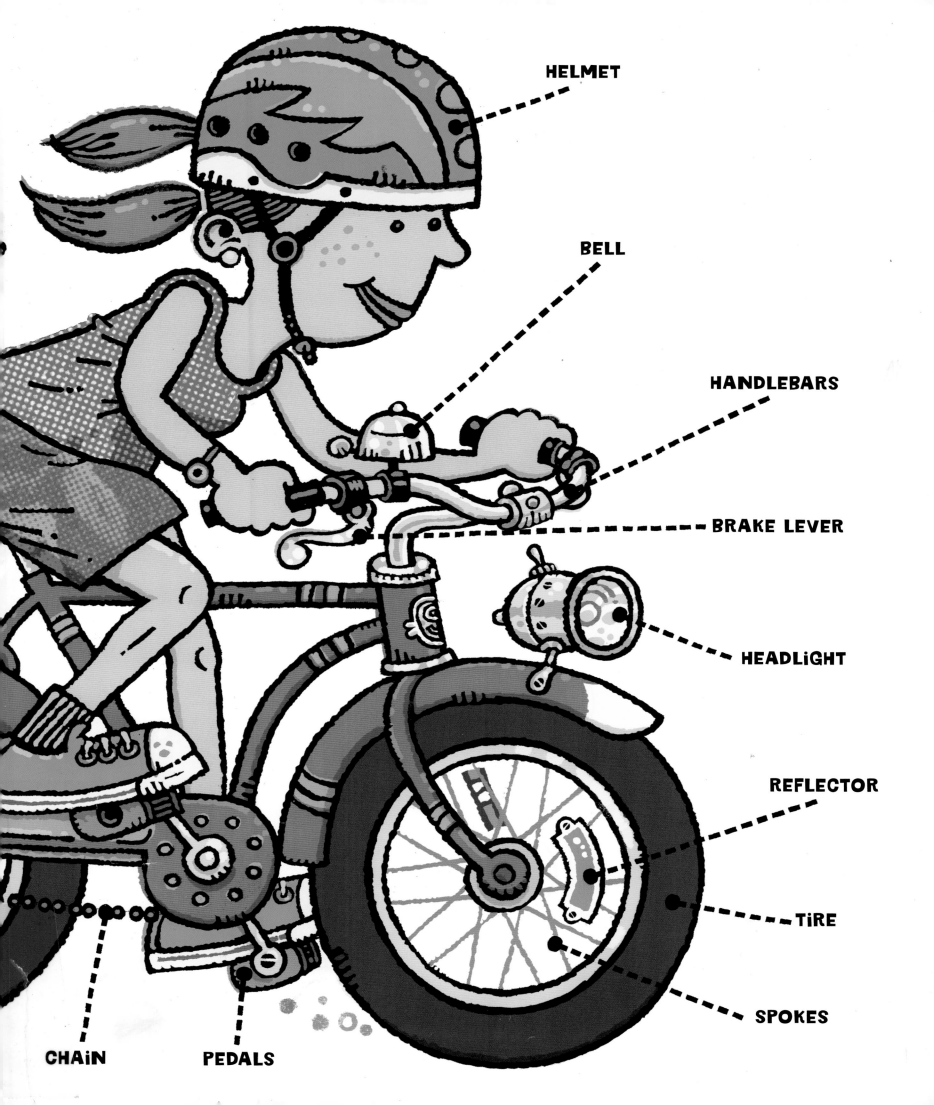

HELMET

BELL

HANDLEBARS

BRAKE LEVER

HEADLIGHT

REFLECTOR

TIRE

SPOKES

CHAIN

PEDALS

That's right, and like cars, motorcycles have motors and need batteries and gas.

And helmets?

Sure, for safety. Now we're almost there . . .

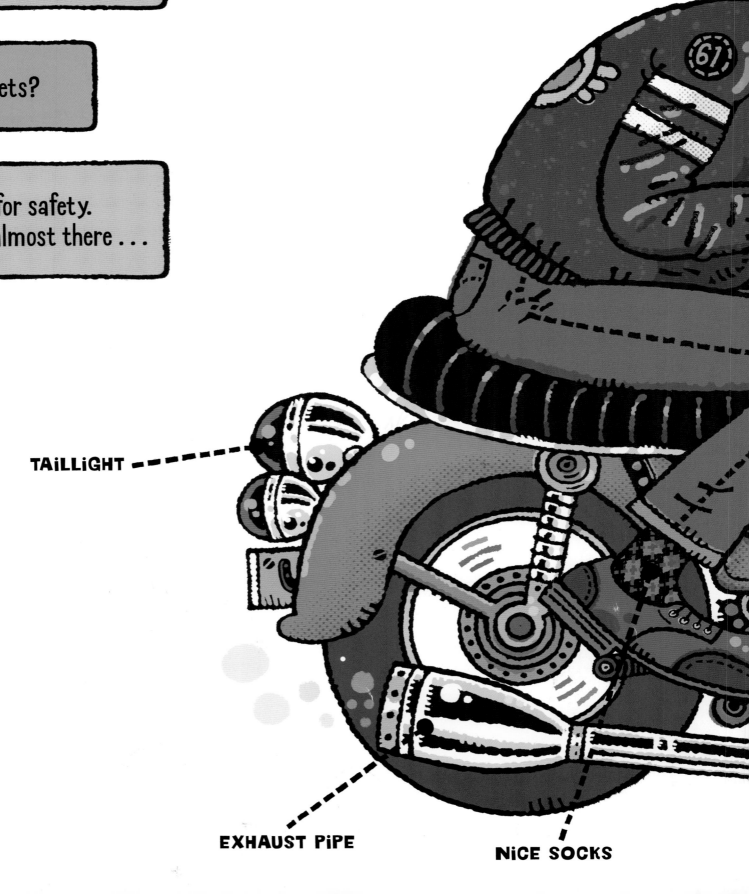

TAILLIGHT

EXHAUST PIPE

NICE SOCKS

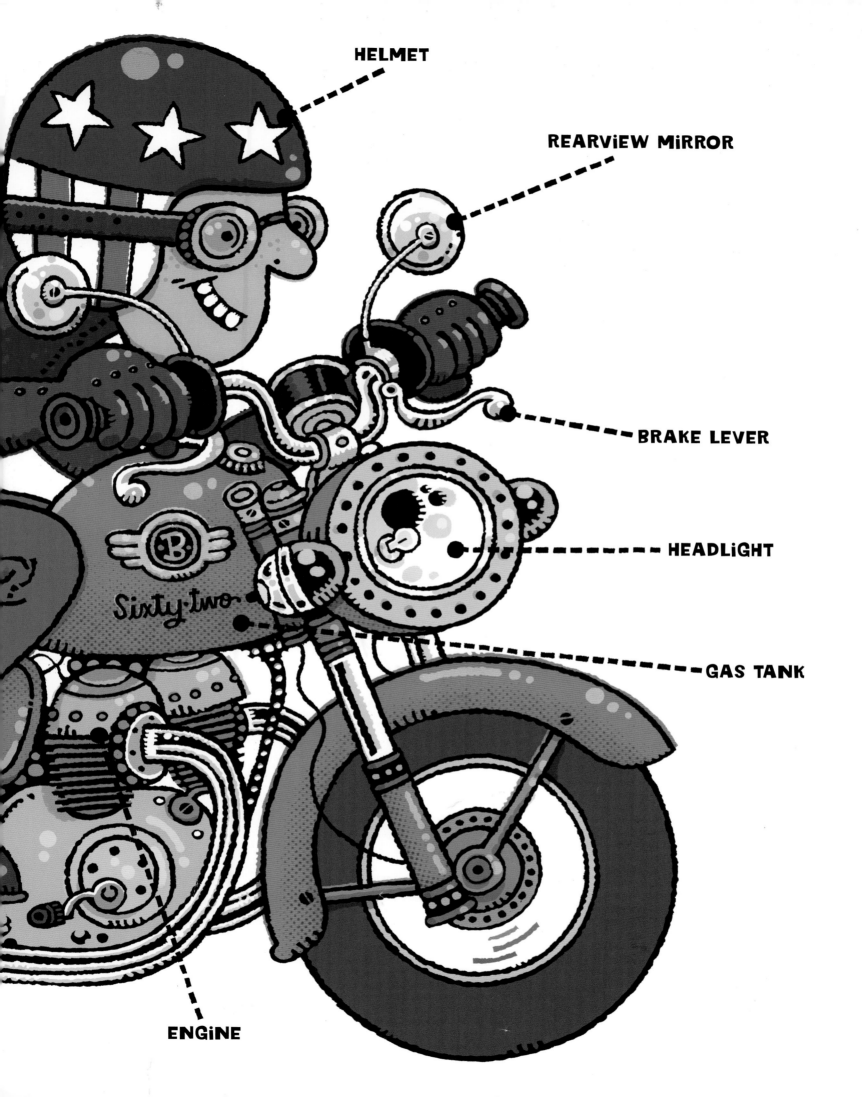

HELMET

REARVIEW MIRROR

BRAKE LEVER

HEADLIGHT

GAS TANK

ENGINE

The subway is a system of trains that run in tunnels below the ground. Like buses, they can take a lot of people where they need to go all over the city. Sometimes you'll see a subway on tracks aboveground, too, on what's called an elevated line.
HEY
MAP
Does this train go downtown?
Nope.
Oh, great.
72
73
SUBWAY TRAIN